To charlotte with Love from Grandma X

Dedicated
to my Beautiful Granddaughter
Ruby.
My inspiration for this story

Fluttabee Tales

Ruby Goes Over the Wall

Book One

GW00646733

Written by Ruth Jones

Illustrated by Patricia Goff

This book belongs to

....

ISBN 978-1-7398048-0-0

<u>**Contents**</u>

Have you ever wondered about the bees that live in your garden or fly around your local area?

Have you looked at their colours and shapes?

Have you thought where they come from or where they go to?

Well, you may be surprised to know that they have family and friends just like you and me. They might have names, characters of their own, and have adventures..........

Chapter 1

M's Fluttadale Bees

In the depths of Yorkshire, hidden away in a quiet rocky valley, lies a beautiful garden. It is filled with wonderful colours from the flowers, changing throughout the four seasons.

Even in winter this special garden gives splashes of colour to brighten a cold, wet, misty day in the valley of Fluttadale.

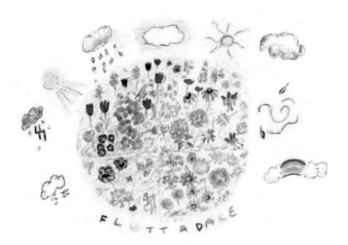

The garden is sheltered from the weather by a tall stone wall. This goes all around the garden.

Inside this wall, you will find a tiny pink cottage, a magical bee hive, and a babbling brook which flows through the centre of this beautiful garden.

But who lives in this cottage you might ask?

Can you guess?

No, it's not a princess, or a fairy, or even a witch, but an old lady called 'M'.

Nobody knows her real name. 'M' is the only person who lives in this part of the small valley of Fluttadale and she is very happy living there on her own.

She does not have a TV, or the internet, or a smart phone, so knows very little of what goes on outside of her beautiful valley. Except what her visitors tell her.

And that suits her just fine.

Her world is her cottage, her garden, her pets and of course, her bees.

In this garden stands a hive, in this hive live her bees.

The Magical Fluttabees.

Chapter 2

<u>Who Are the Fluttabees</u>?

Fluttabees are very special magical bees, a mix of butterfly and bee. Only to be found in Fluttadale. They live in M's hive, ruled by Diamond, their Queen Bee.

Diamond cares for all her Fluttabees. Making them feel safe and loved.

She is very beautiful, her wings and body sparkle like diamonds. This makes everything around her glow in a magnificent sparkling shower of coloured light.

Quite magical!

Can you imagine how it must feel to sparkle
and shimmer like DIAMOND.

There are four families of magical Fluttabees in the hive.

Each family uses their magic to control their own natural element. These elements are
FIRE, WATER, AIR and EARTH.

The Fire family are each coloured shades of red.

The Water family are each coloured shades of blue.

The Air family are each coloured blends of blue, white, yellow and pink.

The Earth family are each coloured shades of green and brown.

The Fluttabee families work together to help keep the garden and the hive at their very best. Everyone works in harmony as a team.

They lead a gentle, quiet, but busy life.
All is good in M's beautiful garden.

But Wait ! One Fluttabee is not having a good start to the day.

Chapter 3

Ruby the Fluttabee

Ruby wakes up in a bad mood, she'd had scary dreams about fire and dragons.

This had kept her awake half the night. To top it all, because she had been tossing and turning in bed, her hair is all tangled.

Oh, her beautiful long red hair, which
normally shines like a ruby and orange flame
in the sunlight.

'What a mess ' Ruby cries.

Tears of hurt and frustration run down her cheeks as her mother tries to pull a brush through her knotted hair.

'Grit your teeth Ruby' she tells herself over and over again.

Until her hair is finally untangled.

She jumps for joy and flies straight out into the garden, blowing kisses to her mother.

Shouting "Thank you" and "Goodbye" in the same breath.

Ruby loves life.

To run, to jump, to skip, but most of all to fly as fast and as high as she can.

She loves the feel of the wind in her hair and on her wings. To feel the warmth of the sun on her shimmering red body and the thrill of going fast and being daring.

She is a beautiful sight to see.

Can you imagine it?

A dazzling, bright ruby red Fluttabee. With shining red and orange coloured hair streaming behind her as she flies through the sky. Turning this way and that, flying up high and swooping down low, laughing with pure enjoyment in these moments.

OH, TO BE FREE. TO FLY LIKE RUBY.

Chapter 4

<u>Adventurous Ruby</u>

Ruby flies through the garden, landing
on her favourite flower the red dahlia.

As Ruby eagerly looks around for her
friends, she tosses her head to send her
hair flowing backwards.

She flutters her wings, and her eyes, as she notices Opal flying towards her. Ruby may like to have lots of fun and be daring, but she also likes to look her best. Being clean and tidy are important to her.

Ruby and Opal flutter their wings and eyes at each other. This is the traditional greeting for Fluttabees, their sign of friendship and love.

They quickly catch up on their latest news, and are soon ready to plan today's adventure.

Ruby, being the daring one, suggests they fly to the very top of the tallest flowering bush in the garden, the buddleia bush. Ruby sees the bush hangs over the garden wall.

'We can look over the wall to see what is happening outside in the valley' says Ruby.

Opal being the cautious Fluttabee isn't certain it's right going outside the garden. What dangers might there be? Diamond, their Queen, and the leaders of the Fluttabees families, do not encourage this.

What would you do?

Go and look, or stay well inside the garden where you know it is safe?

This can be a difficult choice for young Fluttabees.

You and your friends may also have to make difficult choices in your own lives.

Are you Ruby or are you Opal????

Today, Ruby's curiosity and love of adventure get the better of her. She flies straight to the buddleia bush and sits on the top branch and flower.

What a wonderful view.

So different to their garden. The view seems to go on forever.

Ruby is so excited. She squeals with delight.

Opal, on hearing Ruby, decides to join her. As Ruby is still inside the garden, she accepts she is not going out of bounds. Really!

Even though the flower Ruby is sitting on hangs over the wall.

Opal is also amazed and delighted by the view.

The sights and colours are different.

White from the limestone rocks that help form the sides of the valley.

Blue from the brook and the sky.

Grey from the drystone walls that break up the green grass and the trees.

Just like a patchwork quilt.

Mesmerising.

The excited Fluttabees watch how the sun and clouds make shadows on the land. Changing the shades of colour simply by the change in light from sunny to cloudy.

They delight at how the wind blows the branches and leaves in the huge trees, making the trees come alive like strange creatures. The brook is much larger outside the garden and the water almost seems to laugh as it races over the rocks.

Is that Ruby's mum calling?

They quickly fly down to meet her.

'Where have you been?

Your teachers have been asking about you.
You should have been in class half an hour
ago' says Ruby's mum.

'Oh we are sorry, we were busy, and didn't
realise the time. We will go straight to school.'

'Thank you for coming to get us' reply Opal and Ruby together, as they quickly fly away.

'That was close' says Ruby, 'I'm sure my mum will question me later, but now we must get to class before we get into any more trouble.'

'See you later Opal.'

Ruby flies off as fast as her wings will carry her across the garden towards the hive. WHOOSH - swooping down and flying into her classroom.

Although she tries her best, Ruby finds it hard to concentrate. Her mind keeps drifting back to the scene she had seen earlier over the wall. She is determined that once she has finished class she is going back to take another look.

Ruby and her friends normally meet up after class, but today she makes her excuses and flies straight to the buddleia bush. This time she sees lots of large strange white and black fluffy creatures in the fields, they seem to be eating the grass.

What can they be?

Do you know?

Yes, they are sheep. But of course Ruby has never seen a sheep before. She is fascinated, not only do they make noises munching on the grass, but every now and again they baa to each other.

Obviously, it's their language for talking to one another, similar to how Ruby and her family talk through their high pitched buzzing sounds. You and your friends use words.

As she watches, she realises that one small sheep, just below her, seems to be baaing more than the others. In fact the baas seem to be getting louder and louder and more anxious. A larger sheep wanders over, nudges the baby sheep gently, while baaing back.

A baby sheep is called a lamb.
Is the larger sheep the lamb's mother?
What do you think?

After a while, Ruby realises the lamb is still baaing anxiously. The lamb's mother seems to be trying to pull something from her baby's back.

The lamb appears to be stuck to the wall. But how?

The mother is struggling with whatever is holding her lamb to the wall. Ruby being the lively curious one, suddenly flies down to see for herself. Never thinking she is flying out of the garden.

At that moment, elsewhere in the garden, her friends have finished playing and are wondering what Ruby is up to. Opal suggests Ruby could be back on the buddleia bush. They decide to check out this exciting new interest.

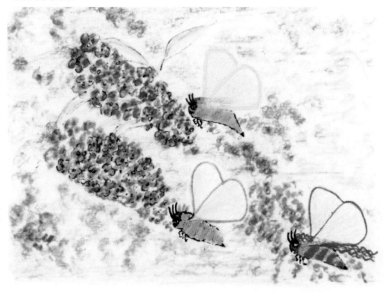

Ruby meanwhile, has investigated the situation with the sheep and can see the lamb's woolly coat is caught in a thick branch growing out of the wall. The mother can't untangle her lamb from the branch.

But Ruby has an idea………..

Being part of the family of FIRE, she has special powers to use the natural element of FIRE. As a very young FIRE Fluttabee, Ruby only knows the very simple skills of using her FIRE. Does she know enough to help the lamb?

She's sure she does, so she quickly trains the fire jet in her tail onto the branch and releases a small flame of fire.

The branch quickly catches alight and burns away the smaller twigs on the branch. The lamb is free.

But what is that?? Smoke coming from the lamb's woolly coat.

Chapter 5

What has Ruby Done?

Ruby only knew she could set fire to wood, she hadn't learnt that other materials can burn too.

Oh dear, what can she do now. She looks on at the lamb and it's mother, neither seem to realise the problem at the moment.

But they soon will.

What if she can't stop the fire from spreading……. What has she done???

She was only trying to help.

Up on top of the buddleia bush the three friends are searching for Ruby. There is no sign of her. They are just about to fly away, when they hear noises from below.

Ruby is crying near two strange creatures. Is she in danger? Emerald, who likes to think he is brave, is the first to act. He flies down to rescue Ruby.

But she doesn't need rescuing from the creatures, quite the opposite, it is the lamb who needs rescuing.

And Emerald knows just what to do.

Only last week he learnt in a lesson how to put out a fire.

He quickly uses his magical EARTH powers to pick up pieces of soil and drops them on the smoke in the lamb's woolly coat.

He goes back and forth moving the earth until he has enough on the lamb's coat to put out the fire.

Following his training he knows he must only use his powers to help others.

Sapphire who has now joined them, blasts the lamb's woolly coat with water to help stop the fire spreading elsewhere. She is from the WATER family so Sapphire has used her magical powers to move water from the brook.

Although the lamb is very confused by what is happening, it senses the danger is over, and skips off to the main flock to tell the tale to family and friends.

Ruby, Emerald and Sapphire look at each other and smile. Ruby thanks them for coming to rescue the lamb and from saving her from causing a real disaster.

Together they fly back to Opal, chattering excitedly about their adventure.

As they fly back into the garden,
Opal the cautious Fluttabee, warns
Ruby about her reckless behaviour
and the consequences
of her choices.

Ruby knows her mistakes, and
understands she must think more carefully
before she acts.

But secretly, she also knows she loved the
excitement of the adventure, and knows she
wants more.......

WOW..... wasn't Ruby lucky her friends were there to help her.

They had used their special, magical powers to help each other and of course help the lamb.

Thankfully the Fluttabees worked together as a team to solve the problem, which resulted in a happy ending.

What can you learn from this story?

Ruby's Wish

That you have fun, love life, be kind, and help people.

But think carefully first.

Make sure you know what you are doing.

Make sure your actions are not going to cause even more problems.

Always try to get help if you are not certain.

NEVER TOUCH OR USE FIRE
ON YOUR OWN.

LEAVE FIRE TO AN ADULT.

THINK BEFORE YOU ACT.

Take Care and Best Wishes from Ruby

Ruby's Little Challenges

1. Look on a map of England. Can you find where the Yorkshire Dales are?

2. Decide where in the Dales you would like the fictional Fluttadale to be.

3. Draw the house you would like to live in if you could live in Fluttadale.

4. Find out which type of real bees live in beehives.

5. If you could make up a special language to communicate with the Fluttabees,
   a] what might you call it?
   b] what are some of the words, or sounds or actions you might create.

6. Find out about the buddleia bush - the colours of the flowers, time of year it grows in Britain, how big it can grow.

Fluttadale
House?

HAVE FUN!

Real Bees/
Beehive?

Yorkshire
Dales?

Buddleia/Flowers/
Size/Colours?

Fluttabees
Words/Sounds?

Thank you for reading
'Ruby goes over the Wall'

We hope you enjoyed our book.
Have fun watching the bees near you.

We would love to hear from you.
Perhaps send us a drawing of a bee you
have seen.
You can reach us on
fluttabeetales@hotmail.com

Look out for the next Fluttabee Tale
'A Stranger Comes to the Garden'

Best wishes
Ruth and Patricia

Printed in Great Britain
by Amazon